Broomstick Rescues

Mabel and Ethel grabbed the broomsticks and jumped on. "I feel an idiot on a broomstick in my swimsuit," grumbled Mabel.

"Never mind about that," said Aunt Myfanwy Magic. "Just follow me as fast as you can fly."

"What's all this about?" yelled Ethel, trying to make herself heard above the wind.

"People stranded by the tide," shouted Aunt Myfanwy Magic. Just pray that we get there in time."

Ann Jungman

Broomstick Rescues

Illustrated by Lynne Chapman

To Sophie with love

Scholastic Children's Books,
Commonwealth House, 1-19 New Oxford Street,
London WC1A 1NU, UK
a division of Scholastic Ltd
London ~ New York ~ Toronto ~ Sydney ~ Auckland
Mexico City ~ New Delhi ~ Hong Kong

Published in the UK by Scholastic Ltd, 1999

Text copyright © Ann Jungman, 1999
Illustrations copyright © Lynne Chapman, 1999

ISBN 0 439 01137 X

Printed by Cox & Wyman Ltd, Reading, Berks.

2 4 6 8 10 9 7 5 3 1

Chapter 1

The Advertisement

"What shall I write for our advertisement?" Ethel asked her sister Mabel.

"Oh, I don't know, something like:

> # WANTED:
>
> Two young assistants to help Broomstick Services with their deliveries of food on broomsticks. Applicants need not have previous experience of broomstick riding but need to have strong nerves and be able to cope with heights.
>
> Apply Ethel or Mabel Witch No. 176 The Towers 0181 573 112

How does that sound?"

"Sounds good. Now where do you think we should put it?" asked Ethel.

"We'll stick it up in the shops and in the club in the flats, and then we'll just wait and see who gets in touch. Come on, we'll go and do it now."

So the two witches flew out of the window and down to the ground and began to stick up their advertisement all over the place.

Just as it was beginning to get dark they put their last notice up and stood back to admire their handiwork. "If I say so myself, Ethel, they do look very fine."

"Couldn't agree more," chortled Mabel. "And with a bit of luck we'll get loads of replies, pick the ones we like best, teach them how to deal with the broomsticks and then we can put our feet up."

"Yes," nodded her sister. "And take it easy."

"Maybe we could even go away on a holiday."

"A holiday!" cried Ethel, her eyes growing as big as saucers. "Could we really go away on a trip?"

"Don't see why not," said Mabel happily.

"Well, *I* do," came an angry voice from behind them.

The two witches turned round to see their sister Maud standing glaring at them with her hands on her hips. "Now what exactly do you two moth-eaten maggots think you are doing?"

"No need to be rude, Maud," replied Mabel, shifting from one foot to the other. "Ethel and I are exhausted and need a break."

"Yes," agreed Ethel in a whisper. "We need to take it easy for a while."

"And why do you need to take it easy?" thundered Maud.

"We've worked very hard, Maud," argued Mabel. "Very hard indeed."

"We set up Broomstick Services to deliver food," said Ethel.

"And then Broomstick Removals to move things," added Mabel. "And now we are tired and want a break."

"I see," said their sister, her eyes narrowing. "So just because you two are a bit tired you plan to let any Tom, Dick or Harry ride around on our broomsticks!"

"Not *any* Tom, Dick or Harry," protested Mabel. "We'll be very fussy about who we take. We'll interview all the applicants very carefully."

"No you won't," declared Maud, "because there won't be any applicants. I have ripped down all your loathsome little notices and will rip down any more you decide to put up. May I remind you that those brooms belonged to our grandmother Merlina the Great and wicked Great-Aunt Morgana."

"So!" cried Mabel defiantly. "Big deal! They've both been dead for ages and I'm sure they wouldn't mind a bit."

"Who knows," added Ethel, "they might even like the idea."

"Like the idea!" yelled Maud, stamping her foot and waving her fist in her sisters' faces. "Have you two gone completely mad? Have you finally lost all your senses? I simply cannot believe I am hearing all this nonsense. What poor dear Mother would have thought I hate to think."

"I don't know why *you're* getting so

high and mighty about a couple of broomsticks," protested Mabel. "I mean, you've more or less given up witchcraft."

"You know perfectly well, Mabel, that when a witch marries an ordinary human being, she has to give up some of her magic, but that does not mean that I do not still respect our ancient rites and tradition. So you can just forget all this nonsense or it will be the worse for you!" And she stormed back into the flats.

Ethel and Mabel stuck their tongues out at her departing back. When Maud turned back to them for a moment, they both smiled at her sweetly.

"You haven't heard the last of this, you lazy good-for-nothings, and don't think you have."

"No, Maud," her sisters said together meekly.

As soon as Maud was gone Ethel got out a notice and Mabel the glue.

"We've still got one left," whispered Mabel.

"Do you think we should?" asked Ethel. "Maud really is very cross."

"Oh pooh!" sniffed Mabel. "We don't have to take any notice of her just because she gets so angry and rude. Let's show her that she can't just boss us around. Come on, Ethel, give me that notice and a pen."

"Why a pen?"

"Because I am going to write on this notice: 'Maud need not apply.'"

Maud need not apply

"Oh Mabel, you wouldn't dare."

"Just you watch me," said Mabel. "Not dare indeed!"

So they stuck up the notice.

"Why don't we go and hide behind that wall?" suggested Ethel. "And then we can watch and see if Maud comes."

"All right," agreed Mabel. So they stood behind the wall and waited. It began to rain but they still waited.

"She's not coming," shivered Mabel. "Let's go home."

"No, someone's coming; I can hear them."

Suddenly a rat raced past. Mabel and Ethel put their hands over their mouths so as not to scream.

"I'm out of here," said Mabel. "If there are rats around, I'm going."

"Shush!" cried Ethel. "Here comes Maud."

Maud strode over to the notice and pulled it off the wall, then she laughed her worst witch laugh and cackled, "So much for your holiday, sisters dear. There is no way you are going to get past me!"

Chapter 2

Rudolfo

Mabel and Ethel slumped in their chairs and sipped their tea miserably. "We'll never get our holiday if Maud has her way," sniffed Ethel.

"We won't let her get her way," declared Mabel. "We'll put an ad in the local paper. Maud doesn't read it. She won't know until it's too late."

"Hee, hee," giggled Ethel. "Won't she get a shock when she wakes up and finds us gone? Oh, I wish I could be here to see it."

"No, you don't," said her sister quickly. "You know how terrifying Maud is when she's angry but we'll be miles away. Now let's ring up the *Plonkford Gazette* and put in our advertisement."

So the same advertisement went in the paper that had been pasted up all over the estate.

On Wednesday, the day the *Plonkford Gazette* came out, Ethel crept over to the newsagent, bought a copy of the paper, slipped it inside her hat and returned to the flats. Looking up she thought she saw Maud's curtains flick a little.

Mabel looked up from cooking eggs and bacon. "Did she see you?"

"I'm not sure but there it is on page seven under 'Situations Vacant'."

"Good," grinned Mabel. "Now sit down and eat your breakfast and then we'll just sit here and wait for our calls."

Just then there was a loud ring at the door bell. Ethel and Mabel looked at each other. "You answer it," whispered Ethel.

"No, you," hissed Mabel.

"What will we do if it's Maud?"

"We'll say we've advertised for a cleaner to help out twice a week here. Now go on, open up."

At that moment another long loud ring rang out.

Ethel grabbed a towel and went to the door. "Sorry, Maud dear," she cried as she let her sister in. "I was just in the bathroom."

"Yes, and I was dishing up the breakfast," added Mabel.

"No problem," said Maud, smiling dangerously sweetly. "I just felt like a cup of tea so I came over."

"So glad you did, Maud, dear," cried Mabel, as she handed Maud a steaming cup of tea. At that moment the phone rang. Mabel and Ethel looked at each other.

"If neither of you is going to answer the phone I will," announced Maud.

"No, no," shouted Mabel. "I'll take it!" and she picked up the receiver. "Hello? Yes, the post is still vacant. Good. Well, come for an interview at no. 176 The Towers."

"We are getting a cleaner," Ethel explained to Maud. "I mean, it's all getting too much; we can't do everything, you know."

"I see," nodded Maud, with another of her sweet smiles. "What a good idea. I wonder how many people will apply for the job?"

After that the phone rang several times and the witches arranged interviews at half-hour intervals. Maud sat and drank several cups of tea, smiling all the time, and then got up to go.

"Well, sisters, I hope you find yourselves a very good cleaner and thank you so much for the tea. See you soon. Byeee!"

The moment the door closed Mabel and Ethel collapsed in giggles. "I don't think she suspected a thing."

"No, nothing at all."

On the dot of three p.m. the bell rang and Mabel opened the door to a bright-looking young woman. "Come on in. Would you like a cup of tea?"

"That would be nice," said the girl.

Ethel made the tea and asked the girl as she poured it, "How do you feel about riding around on a broomstick?"

Suddenly the girl let out a terrible scream and ran out of the front door. Ethel and Mabel looked down and there, coming out of the teapot, was a stream of lively green frogs. "Maud!" they cried together. "She *did* guess."

"Maybe we shouldn't offer the others tea," suggested Mabel. "We'll just go straight into the interview."

"Good idea," agreed Mabel. "That'll show her."

But it didn't work. The next one who came ran screaming from the flat after a huge black spider crawled up her leg, and the next fainted when a snake slid over his shoulder.

Ethel and Mabel sat at opposite sides of the table. "We'd better just cancel all the others," groaned Mabel.

"I agree," sighed Ethel. "But how did Maud find out?"

"I smell a rat," groaned Mabel.

"No you do not!" came an indignant voice from the floor.

The witches looked down and saw a rat looking at them indignantly, with his arms angrily folded in front of him.

"You *are* a rat!" declared Mabel. "Why deny it?"

"I'm not denying it," cried the rat. "But you did not smell me. I am wearing the very latest rat aftershave and smell as fresh as a daisy. Smell a rat indeed!"

"We didn't mean we'd smelled a rat in that sense. What we meant was that someone told Maud about us."

"Oh yes, that was me all right," the rat assured them. "Yes, it certainly was. Rudolfo the rat at your service, ladies. Maud said that if I didn't come here and tell her everything that was going on, she would do something really terrible to me."

"Really terrible?" questioned Mabel.

"Yes, really, really, terrible; I can't even bear to think about it." And the rat wiped his brow and tried hard not to cry.

"What?" asked Ethel and Mabel together.

"She said she would turn me into a human being. Can you imagine that? Oh dear, it just doesn't bear thinking about."

"Would that be *so* terrible?" asked Ethel.

"Terrible? It most certainly would. I mean, walking around on two legs and without any fur and being too big to swim in the sewers! Oh dear, I just tremble at the thought."

"Do you realize that we are witches too, Rudolfo? And that we could turn you into a human as easily as Maud?"

"I know, but you two are nice and kind. You wouldn't do that to poor old Rudolfo now, would you? Anyway, you haven't got any of the magic books. She's made sure of that."

"True," mumbled Mabel gloomily.

"What we are going to do next I do not know," grumbled Ethel. "Maud has wrecked all our plans as usual."

Just then the phone rang.

"It'll be her. Let's pretend we're out," cried Mabel.

"No point," Rudolfo told them. "She's at her window watching with her binoculars. Look."

Mabel sighed and picked up the phone. "Broomstick Services. How can I help you?"

"Good afternoon, sisters dear," came Maud's silky voice. "I wonder if I might trouble you to come over here for tea. Some old friends have just dropped in and want to see you."

"That's very kind, Maud, but we're both rather tired. Another time maybe?"

"No, now, and you tell Rudolfo that if he wants to go on being a rat to get you over here."

"Nothing for it," grumbled Mabel. "We'd better go and face the music. Come on, Ethel; come on, Rudolfo."

The two sisters looked round for the rat but he had already gone.

"He really is scared of Maud, isn't he?" commented Mabel.

"Me too," confessed Ethel.

"I don't blame him either. Now come on," said her sister, taking her arm. "Come on, we'll just go over and face the music together."

Chapter 3

Three Aunts

Gingerly the sisters and the rat approached Maud's door. They were just about to knock when it was flung open and Rudolfo raced in ahead of the two witches.

"Ethel, Mabel, my dear sisters, welcome, welcome. Do come on in."

Nervously Ethel and Mabel went into

the room and there, sitting in a circle, all dressed up in full witch gear, were three of their great-aunts.

"There they are, the two sinners. Oh, you bad, bad girls!" cried Aunt Morag McCracken. "As soon as Maud told me what you two were up to I leapt on my broomstick and came all the way down from Scotland. Och aye, I had to; there was no a minute to waste. How could you two even think of loaning out our ancient witch brooms? Whatever were you two lassies thinking of?"

"Sorry, Aunt Morag," whispered Ethel and Mabel, looking at the floor.

"Well, you two come over here this minute and say hello to your Aunt Molly Murphy," said a jolly plump figure.

"Hello, Aunt Molly," cried Mabel, leaning to give her a kiss on one cheek, while Ethel kissed her on the other cheek. "How did you come to be here?"

"The moment Maud phoned I got on my broom and came directly across the

Irish Sea, so I did. It was very rough too, I don't mind telling you, but I said to meself, 'Rain or no rain, wind or no wind, when there are witches selling out and when those witches are my very own great-nieces, Molly Murphy, your duty is to get to England as soon as poss.' Well, it was the least I could do in memory of my dear sister Merlina."

"Well, it's wonderful to see you Aunt Molly Murphy," Ethel told her.

"Well, it's nice to see you two as well, so it is, but I wish the circumstances were happier."

"Sorry, Aunt Molly," sniffed Ethel. "Mabel and I didn't mean to do anything bad, we just wanted a break from working for Broomstick Services for a while."

"That's as maybe, darling, but you

must never, never let a mere mortal use your broomsticks. Honest to goodness, that is not at all what witches are supposed to do."

"So sorry," wept Ethel. "We didn't mean to cause all this trouble, really we didn't."

"Of course you didn't, dear," came a gentle lilting voice, and there stood Aunt Myfanwy Magic smiling at them.

"Oh, Aunt Myfanwy Magic!" cried Mabel. "Thank goodness you are here."

"Don't bother thanking goodness," came Maud's sour voice. "Thank me!"

"Yes, Maud dear," said Aunt Myfanwy Magic, as she hugged first Mabel and then Ethel. "But speaking for myself, I am delighted to have a break from my Welsh hills and all the mist from the mountains and the sea."

"I hope you realize that you have caused the great-aunts much inconvenience with your dreadful behaviour," thundered Maud.

"Aye, a disgrace to witches everywhere," agreed Aunt Morag McCracken.

"That's right, a disgrace they are," echoed Aunt Molly Murphy. "Lending brooms to all and sundry! Never heard the like, no not in all my born days."

"We only wanted a bit of a holiday," sniffled Ethel.

"Yes," said Mabel. "We've been flying around delivering food for years and we need a break. We're exhausted."

"Witches don't get exhausted," declared Aunt Morag McCracken. "And witches don't need holidays."

"We do," insisted Mabel and Ethel.

"Will you just listen to the two of them! A holiday indeed!" cried Aunt Molly Murphy indignantly. "Oh Maud, my poor darling girl – how do you cope with these two? No wonder you had to send for the great-aunts with more experience than you."

Maud's eyes flashed dangerously. "What shall I do with them, Auntie?

Shall I turn them into toads or rats? Yes, rats would be good, then they could keep Rudolfo company.

"NO!" yelled Rudolfo, Ethel, Mabel, Aunt Morag McCracken, Aunt Molly Murphy and Aunt Myfanwy Magic at once.

"Why not?" demanded Maud. "I've got the spell right here:

"To turn a person to a rat,
A bit of fly, a bit of bat,
Put it all into a hat,
Swish it round and that is that."

"Now, Maud," said Aunt Myfanwy Magic. "This is all going a bit far."

"Have you got a better idea?" growled Maud.

"Oh my goodness, I certainly have," smiled the Welsh witch. "Now, as you know I live in a castle, on a mountain overlooking the sea, and it is very lovely, but sometimes I do get just the tiniest bit lonely."

"Oh, poor Aunt Myfanwy," said Ethel and Mabel sympathetically.

"Yes," continued Aunt Myfanwy Magic. "So I was wondering if I could persuade the two of you to come and stay with me for a bit of a holiday, like."

Big grins spread over Ethel and Mabel's faces. "Oh, Aunt Myfanwy, we would love to."

"Huh!" sniffed Maud. "And what about Broomstick Services, then?"

"I was hoping the three of you could take over for a couple of weeks," said Aunt Myfanwy. "And that nice little girl who was here earlier, she seemed very promising."

"Oh, you mean Jackie," said Ethel. "Yes, she's very keen to be a witch."

"That's right," continued Aunt Myfanwy. "And I thought Morag and Molly might like to have a bit of a change, like, and spend a few weeks in town, and you know the ropes, Maud dear."

"Is it a kind of working holiday are you thinking of?" demanded Aunt Molly Murphy.

"Yes, and then you might like to come and stay with me in Wales for a while, for a more relaxing break."

"I'm no working for nothing," declared Aunt Morag McCracken fiercely.

"You can keep all the profits," Mabel assured her.

"Now you're talking," said Aunt Morag McCracken and gave one of her very rare smiles.

"You could stay in our place while we're away, aunts," offered Ethel.

"Well, it seems we have organized a very nice compromise," smiled Aunt Myfanwy. "Ethel and Mabel will come with me and Broomstick Services will carry on as usual."

"I hope someone is going to thank me for saving the situation," grumbled Maud. "If I hadn't stepped in and taken strong action, some very undesirable goings-on might have taken place."

"Yes, thank you for all the trouble you've taken, Maud," said Ethel.

"Glad we sorted out a witchy sort of solution," added Mabel.

"You'd better go," grumbled Maud, "or I might change my mind. I'll be working away here while you two laze on a beach.

Yes, you'd better go right away or I'll get the rat spell out again."

"I'm out of here!" shrieked Rudolfo and he raced out of the door like streaked lightning.

"On to your broomsticks, girls," said Aunt Myfanwy Magic quickly. "Come on, just follow me and enjoy your visit to the town, sisters. Byeee!"

As they flew off they could hear Maud muttering,

"To turn a person to a rat,
A bit of fly, a bit of bat..."

Chapter 4

By the Seaside

"I've never had so much fun," sighed Mabel, as she finished covering her sister with sand.

"Me neither," agreed Ethel, giggling. "It was well worth having a row with Maud for."

"I wonder how the aunts are getting on delivering food?" said Mabel. "When I spoke to Maud on the phone, it all sounded fine."

"Do you think we could just stay down here?" asked Ethel wistfully from her position in the sand. "It's so lovely."

"No," groaned Mabel. "We'll have to go back – that was the deal we made, though I don't much fancy flying around with food for the rest of my life."

"Me neither," agreed Ethel.

Just then Aunt Myfanwy Magic flew in on her broomstick. "Oh, there you are. I had a terrible time finding you. Here's some fresh lemonade and some homemade ice-cream."

"Oh, thank you, Aunt Myfanwy Magic," cried the two witches, as Ethel climbed out of her hole. "That's very kind of you." And the three of them sat on the beach and ate and drank.

"It's so perfect here, Auntie," cried Mabel. "Neither of us wants to go back to work."

"Oh dear," replied Aunt Myfanwy Magic, shaking her head, "Well, we'll have to see what we can do about that."

For the rest of the day Aunt Myfanwy Magic sat in her room, looking out of the window and thinking hard. "I've got to do something to get those two silly girls back to work," she told her cat. "Can't have them living down here for ever, doing nothing; they've got an important job to do back home."

The cat smiled and went and sat on a bright red cover of a book of spells. Aunt Myfanwy Magic picked up the cat and opened the book. "Which page, pussy?" she asked.

The cat wriggled free and started to

turn the pages of the book until she found what she wanted: "DISASTERS".

"1. Cut off by High Tide," read out Aunt Myfanwy. "Thank you, cat, I think I can follow the way your mind is working. Yes, I think that will do very nicely, very nicely indeed."

The next day Mabel and Ethel were busy making a sand castle, when Aunt Myfanwy Magic flew in carrying both their broomsticks. "Come on quickly!" she cried. "Grab your broomsticks, quick, it's urgent!"

Mabel and Ethel grabbed the broomsticks and jumped on. "I feel an idiot on a broomstick in my swimsuit," grumbled Mabel.

"Never mind about that," said Aunt Myfanwy Magic. "Just follow me as fast as you can fly."

"What's all this about?" yelled Ethel, trying to make herself heard above the wind.

"People stranded by the tide," shouted Aunt Myfanwy Magic. "Just pray that we get there in time."

They flew along the coastline and over a big headland.

"Down there," shouted Aunt Myfanwy Magic.

Ethel and Mabel looked down and there trapped on some rocks were a family of five, waving desperately and shouting for help.

"Start the descent," called Aunt Myfanwy Magic. "Look, the waves are lapping at the rock they're standing on. Not a moment to be wasted."

Aunt Myfanwy, followed by Mabel and Ethel, flew down to loud cheers from the family.

"Quick, hop on, children," cried Aunt Myfanwy.

"Are we going on a broomstick?" cried the children. "Whoopee!"

The father lifted two children on to

Aunt Myfanwy Magic's broomstick. Then Mabel flew close to let the mother and other child get on. "Thank you *so* much," they said, with a huge sigh of relief, as they scrambled on board.

Finally, Ethel swooped and grabbed the father seconds before he was carried out to sea by a huge wave. "Boy, am I pleased to see you three," he gasped.

"Another few minutes and we'd have had it."

"Think nothing of it," Ethel told him, glowing with pride. "That is what witches are for. Now where can we take you?"

"Straight to our hotel, please," said the mother. "We need to get these children dry. It's right in the middle of the town, I'm afraid."

"No problem," laughed Ethel and Mabel, forgetting for a minute about their swimming-costumes.

When the three witches and their cargo landed in the town, a huge cheer went up, though some of the children were giggling at the witches.

"Does anyone have a towel or something?" asked Mabel. "I feel a bit of an idiot standing in the middle of a town in my swimming-costume."

Someone rushed forward and put a towel round Mabel and someone else put a blanket round Ethel, and they all marched off to the police station. Once there, there were more congratulations as the police chief and the fire chief and the lifeboat crew all assured them they could never have got there in time.

That night there was a huge party in the town and everyone drank a toast to Ethel and Mabel and Aunt Myfanwy Magic, and there was dancing way into the night. Someone found some fireworks and started to let them off in a narrow street.

Suddenly there was a cry: "Look, a fire!" And someone else shouted, "There are people shouting from the top storeys!"

"Go and get the fire engines!" yelled the fire chief.

"You'll never get to them in time," groaned the chief of police.

"On your broomsticks!" called Aunt Myfanwy Magic, and the three witches flew up to the top floors of the building and hovered while the trapped people climbed on to their broomsticks, and the crowd cheered below.

"We're so grateful," said one of the rescued women, as she was helped to a stretcher. "But all our belongings are up there."

"Don't worry," cried Mabel. "We'll get them for you. Come on, Ethel."

So the two sisters flew in and out till they had every last thing out of the top floor. By the end both the witches had black faces and their clothes and brooms were singed. Everyone crowded round them, patting them on the back and singing their praises.

The mayor shook his head. "How other towns manage without witches I simply do not know, really I don't," he said, and everyone there applauded in agreement. All the local cafés threw open their doors and offered the crowd free breakfast to celebrate all the rescues.

The next day Mabel and Ethel were down on the beach again making a sandcastle.

"I really enjoyed myself yesterday," Mabel told her sister.

"Me too," agreed Ethel. "Saving all those people and being cheered and fêted."

"Funny, 'cos I thought I'd never want to sit on a broomstick again."

"I know, but it's different when you're saving people."

"Maybe we could go home and save people. What do you say to that, Ethel?"

"Well, I don't see why not, I really don't. I mean, there are more people in big cities, so there will be more saving to be done. It seems to me people need saving everywhere, don't they?"

"Well, they do, they're such a dozy lot."

"Yes, I suppose it really is time to think about going back. I mean, Aunt Morag McCracken and Aunt Molly Murphy and Maud may be a bit exhausted. Poor things, they're not experienced at the food delivering like us."

"We'd better go and pack," said Mabel sadly. "Pity, 'cos I really like it here."

"We can always come back," Ethel reminded her.

So they trudged back to Aunt Myfanwy Magic's and put on their witch's clothes and began to pack.

"I think you've made a very wise decision," Aunt Myfanwy told her nieces. "Of course I shall miss you both but I'm sure you will be back for another holiday soon."

Just then the phone rang.

"Don't you worry, we'll be there in a

jiffy," they heard her say. "That was the emergency services, girls. Another job for us. Come on, you two. Rock climbers trapped on a cliff, one of them is hurt. The police think we can get there faster than them."

So the three of them flew off round the coast till they came to a high chalk cliff face. Perched uncomfortably on a ledge were three climbers.

"I've got a stretcher," shouted Aunt Myfanwy Magic. "Take one end each. Hold it steady."

So the climbers put their wounded friend gently on to the stretcher.

"Well done, girls," said the climbers gratefully. "We'd never have been able to get him down on our own."

"Will you two be all right?" asked Aunt Myfanwy Magic in a concerned tone.

"We'll be fine. We'll climb down as fast as we can and go straight to the hospital to check up on our mate."

"See you at the hospital then." And they flew off as fast as they could without hurting the wounded man.

The next night the mayor put on a firework display in honour of the three witches and the whole town turned out to watch and cheer. When it was all over the mayor stood on a table to make a speech.

"Ladies and gentlemen, Ethel, Mabel and Myfanwy, I want to say a very big thank you on behalf of the people of Llangored and all our visitors for the incredible way in which you have helped avoid several big disasters. In fact I can't remember a week in which we have had a flood, a fire and a climbing accident."

Aunt Myfanwy Magic smiled mysteriously and looked up at the night sky.

"And I would like to ask Mabel and Ethel to stay on in Llangored and help the emergency services."

Everyone clapped. Ethel and Mabel looked at each other, then Mabel climbed up on the table next to the mayor.

"My sister and I would like to thank you all for your kind invitation; we really love it here and we are very tempted to stay, particularly as people seem to do so many dangerous things round here. But we have promised Maud and Aunt Morag McCracken and Aunt Molly Murphy to go home. So, reluctantly we will have to leave you. But we'll come back every year for our hols."

"Three cheers for witches!" yelled the crowd. "Three cheers for Ethel and Mabel and Aunt Myfanwy Magic!"

Chapter 5

Broomstick Rescues

After the firework display three very happy witches returned singing to Aunt Myfanwy Magic's castle. As they came in through the door a familiar voice said: "Evening, girls! Glad to see you so happy."

"Rudolfo!" cried Mabel. "What are you doing here?"

"What I am doing here is bringing you a message and an order that it is definitely time for you to be coming home. The others have had enough of delivering food."

"Well, that didn't take them long," sniffed Mabel. "But we were planning to come home anyway."

"Good," sniffed the rat, "because You Know Who said she'd do You Know What to me if I didn't persuade you to return immediately."

"Now what is that rat talking about?" asked gentle Aunt Myfanwy Magic.

"Maud," explained Ethel. "She's always threatening to turn Rudolfo here into a human."

"Oh dear," said Aunt Myfanwy Magic. "Now that wouldn't do at all, would it?"

"It certainly would not," wept the rat.

"So if Ethel and Mabel go back today, will all be well?" asked the witch.

"Yes," nodded Rudolfo. "You see, Maud is expecting and says she can't go flying around here, there and everywhere any more."

"Expecting?" cried Ethel and Mabel together.

"Yes, expecting," said the rat. "You know, a baby; you two are going to be aunties."

"Oh!" cried Aunt Myfanwy Magic, clapping her hands together in delight. "Now isn't that the best news for years? Come on, everyone, off we go, not a moment to be wasted." And the three witches climbed on to their broomsticks.

"Do you want a lift, Rudolfo?" asked Ethel.

"Certainly not," replied the rat. "I'll

run back through the sewers like any self-respecting rat. See you back at the flats and you can explain to herself that I succeeded in my mission, so she won't do You Know What."

"We will," cried Ethel and Mabel, as they rose into the air waving at Rudolfo, who waved back as he dried his tears with his long tail.

The three witches arrived back at the flats well after midnight. Ethel and Mabel flew straight over to Maud's flat and knocked on the window. A very bleary-eyed Maud opened the window.

"What do you two think you are doing? Don't you realize it's the middle of the night and a witch in my condition needs her sleep – or didn't that rotten rat tell you?"

"Oh yes, Maud dear, he did, he did, but we were just so excited we had to come and see you straight away."

"Huh!" sniffed Maud. "At two in the morning indeed. I can see that two weeks away at the seaside hasn't made you any more sensible."

"No, Maud," agreed Ethel, nodding her head. "We just needed to say congratulations and tell you that we are thrilled that we are going to be aunts."

"Good," grumbled Maud. "Now go away." And she slammed the window down angrily.

"She doesn't change," sighed Ethel.

"I know, but maybe motherhood will mellow her," said Mabel. "Come on, back home."

When they got to their flat, they found Aunt Morag McCracken snoring in one bed and Aunt Molly Murphy in another.

Aunt Myfanwy was sleeping peacefully in the only armchair.

"Oh dear," groaned Mabel.

"We'll have to make do with the kitchen chairs," sighed Ethel. "And we'd better be quiet. If we wake the aunts up it'll be worse than Maud."

So the two witches spent an uncomfortable night with their heads on their arms on the kitchen table.

They were woken up by a stern voice saying, "Och, now look at that! Two sleeping witches and me desperate for a wee bit of porridge for my breakfast."

Ethel and Mabel leapt up. "Sorry, Aunt Morag."

"Aye, I should think so. Now one of you wipe the table and the other put on the kettle. Now have you heard the news about Maud?"

"Yes, Auntie. Isn't it wonderful?"

"Aye, and I hope it stops you two lassies from wanting to take holidays all the time."

"Yes, Auntie. Thank you, Auntie."

"Though I have to admit, it was quite fun delivering the food for a while. Now away with you and clean your teeth and I'll get some porridge ready while you're gone."

When they got back to the kitchen there were five steaming big bowls of porridge and Aunt Molly Murphy and Aunt Myfanwy Magic sitting at the table.

Just then there was a knock at the door.

"Maud!" yelled Ethel and Mabel together and rushed to open the door, but there stood Rudolfo, panting.

"Is it all right?" he gasped. "Does she know I told you?"

"She does," Ethel told him. "But we were coming home anyway."

"Don't tell her that, *pleeeeease*," begged the rat, looking tearful again. "Let her think it was all my doing."

"Oh, all right," agreed the two witches. "If you think that will help stop her turning you into a human being."

"It might," sniffled Rudolfo. "It just might, you never know."

"You never know what?" came Maud's voice.

"What it's going to be like to be an auntie," cried Mabel, and flung her arms round Maud while Ethel gave Fred, Maud's husband, a big kiss.

"Yes, the minute we heard the news from Rudolfo we rushed back," said Ethel, giving Fred a big kiss. "We could hardly believe it: us – aunts. What a thrill!"

"I'm glad you're so pleased. Does that mean you'll stay at home from now on?"

"It most certainly does," Mabel told her firmly. "Wild horses wouldn't drag us away. A niece or a nephew, now isn't that a lovely thought?"

"Congratulations to both of you," said Aunt Myfanwy Magic, smiling fondly at Fred and Maud. "And I'm excited too, after all the pleasure my great-nieces have given me. I'm looking forward to the great-great-niece or nephew."

"Did these two great-nieces behave themselves, then?" demanded Maud. "You can tell me; I'm still in the mood to turn them both into rats."

"Oh no," cried Aunt Myfanwy Magic. "They were wonderful – real heroines."

"Heroines? Whatever do you mean?"

At that moment the door bell rang and

there stood a fireman with a bunch of flowers. "Sorry to interrupt," he said, "But I'm looking for Miss Ethel and Miss Mabel."

"That's us," declared the two witches, stepping forward.

"Ladies, can I give you these flowers with the compliments of the Plonkford Fire Station? We got a call from Wales telling us what heroines you were and we were hoping we could call on you in a crisis."

"Of course," agreed the sisters, grinning with pleasure.

"What exactly is going on here?" demanded Maud.

Just then the bell rang again and there stood a policeman clutching a huge box of chocolates. "Could I have a word with the witches Ethel and Mabel?" he asked.

The sisters stepped forward again, pushing the flowers into Maud's hands.

"On behalf of the Plonkford Police Station I would like to give you these chocolates and hope that you will help us out just as you did our colleagues in Wales."

"We certainly will," said the sisters, giggling as they took the chocolates.

"Is someone going to explain all this to me?" snarled Maud in her most frightening voice.

"Well, you see, Maud dear..." began Aunt Myfanwy Magic, when the bell rang yet again. Maud flung it open and there stood two ambulance drivers carrying three bottles of champagne. "Are Ethel and Mabel here?"

"Here we are," cried the two witches,

quickly handing Maud the box of chocolates.

"We've brought this round from the Plonkford Hospital Trust in the hope that you two girls will help us with special cases, just like you did in Wales."

"No problem," the witches told him.

"Now come on in and we'll have a drink and some chocolates. Maud, find a vase for the flowers and give the chocolates here."

So everyone sat round drinking champagne and eating chocolates while Ethel and Mabel told them about their exciting exploits in Wales.

"Huh!" sniffed Maud. "So you went around saving people, did you?"

"Exactly," nodded Ethel.

"That's no way for a witch to behave," grumbled Maud. "Saving people indeed!"

"We had to do it, Maud," explained her sisters. "You would too. And now we're going to be helping out the emergency services here as well."

"Well," said gentle Aunt Myfanwy Magic, smiling. "So everything has worked out very well. Maud is to have a baby and Ethel and Mabel are going to be part-time heroines, the aunts have had a break and done a great job, and Rudolfo is still a rat. Things couldn't have worked out better."

"Open another bottle of champagne," said Mabel, "and let's all drink to that."

So everyone lifted their glasses and Rudolfo sipped his from a saucer.

"To Broomstick Rescues, three great-aunts, a rat and the new baby!"

The End